Tacky

and the Winter Games

HELEN LESTER

Illustrations by LYNN MUNSINGER

Houghton Mifflin Company Boston 2005

Walter Lorraine Books

To the athletic side of my family — Robin, Rob, and Jamie.

— H.L.

Walter Lorraine Books

www.houghtonmifflinbooks.com

Library of Congress Cataloging-in-Publication Data
Lester, Helen.
  Tacky and the Winter Games / by Helen Lester ; illustrated by Lynn Munsinger.
    p. cm.
  "Walter Lorraine Books."
  Summary: Tacky and his fellow penguins on Team Nice Icy Land train hard for the
  Winter Games, but Tacky's antics make their chances of winning a medal seem slim.
  ISBN-13: 978-0-618-55659-5 (hardcover)
  ISBN-10: 0-618-55659-1 (hardcover)
  [1. Winter sports—Fiction. 2. Penguins—Fiction.] I. Munsinger, Lynn, ill. II. Title.
  PZ7.L56285Taau 2005
  [E]—dc22

                                                        2005002282

Printed in the United States of America
WOZ 10 9 8 7 6 5 4 3 2 1

A-huff-and-a-puff-and-a-huff-and-a-puff-and-a-huff-and-a-puff.
"WHAT'S HAPPENING?" blared Tacky the Penguin as he came across
his companions Goodly, Lovely, Angel, Neatly, and Perfect.
"We're"—huff— "training"—puff—they replied.

"Training?" wondered Tacky hopefully. "As in, choo-choo?"
"No. Training. Like athletes. The Winter Games are coming, and we must must must be in shape to win win win."
Looking closely at Tacky—not the fittest of birds—they added, "Let's get going!"

So the penguins trained.

They raced up steep hills.

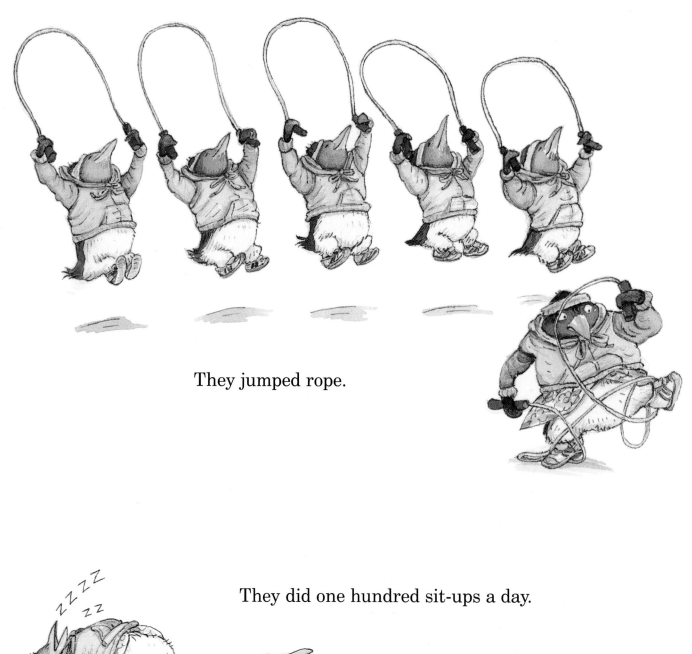

They jumped rope.

They did one hundred sit-ups a day.

ZZZZ
ZZ

They lifted weights.

They rode bikes.

They ate special training meals.

They kept strict training hours.

Most of all, they practiced their events.

Bobsledless racing.

Ski jumping.

Speed skating.

And finally, after weeks of work, Team Nice Icy Land was ready for the long waddle to the Winter Games.

Off they went.

Rat-a-tat-tat. Rat-a-tat-tat.
The athletes marched into the stadium for the Opening Ceremonies.
Teams had come from far and wide.

They came from the Highlands, the Lowlands, the Funlands, and of course, the Nice Icy Land. Rat-a-tat-tat. Rat-a-tat-tat. On they marched. Ratty-tatty-tatty-boomby-ratty-tatty-boom—Hey!

Tacky marched to a different drummer.

For the big show, the penguins all joined in singing the Winter Games Anthem:

The Winter Games Anthem

With our beaks held high and our bellies held low, we'll
do our best in the ice and snow, with a
Yodel waddle ho and a Yodel waddle hee! May the
best team win . . . and let's hope it's we.

After lighting the torch and exchanging high flippers as a sign of friendship, the athletes filed out past the display of medals. Medals to dream about.

The sun rose.
Eager penguins prepared for the first event, the
bobsledless race.
Little webbed feet wrapped around big penguin tummies.
Pop! They were off!

Tacky was way off. Looking at the wonderful hill before him, he cried, "Great for belly sliding!" With that, he charged under his surprised teammates and sped them down, crossing the finish line in record time.

17

But wait.

The official announced, "This is a bobsled*less* race.
You have a bobsled."

Goodly, Lovely, Angel, Neatly, and Perfect tried to explain that
it was not a bobsled: it was a penguin.

18

"Doesn't look much like a penguin," said the official, examining
Tacky. "Not much like a bobsled either. Don't know what it is.
Anyway, no medals for you. Illegal equipment."
So no medals for Team Nice Icy Land. Yet.

In the afternoon the athletes strapped frozen fish on their
feet for the ski jumping event.

While the jumpers waited for their turns, Tacky spent *just* a few
moments in the hut toasting his toes by the fire.

Weren't winter sports wonderful!

Swoop—plop. Swoop—plop. Swoop—plop.
One after another, the athletes made graceful jumps
and lovely landings.
Plippy ploppy plippy ploppy. What was this?

Tacky's fish had become thawed by the warmth of the fire and were now flopping wildly. He made a higher jump than he had intended . . .

and lots . . .

of . . .

landings.

No medals for Team Nice Icy Land. Yet.

That evening the speed skating relay race was the final event. "Last chance, Tacky," warned Goodly, Lovely, Angel, Neatly, and Perfect, who looked mighty aerodynamic in their costumes.

Tacky looked mighty — well — tacky.

The other teams had already finished, and their times
were very fast.
Now it was team Nice Icy Land's turn.

SCOREBOARD

team HIGHLAND	team LOWLAND	team FUNLAND
Hamish ... 1 min.	RUUD ... 1 min.	LOOPY ... ½ min.
Sheena ... 1 min.	Pieter ... ½ min.	Goofy ... 1 min
Andrew ... 2 min.	Lise ... ½ min.	Slapstick ... 1 min.
Morag ... ½ min.	HANS ... 1½ min.	HILARITY ... ½ min
Scott ... 1 min.	Grete ... 1 min.	Giggles ... ½ min
Simon ... 1 min	Joop ... 1 min.	LOONY ... 1 min.
7½	5	4½

FAST!

GOOD!

LOVELY

REALLY
FAST!

WOW
!!!

Pop! Off they went.
One by one, Tacky's companions took a turn
around the rink.

Goodly passed the baton to Lovely.

Who passed the baton to Angel.

Who passed the baton to Neatly.

Who passed the baton to Perfect.

Who passed the baton to Tacky.
Who said, "Thank you" and ate it.

Ate it?

Ate it.

Well, it *looked* like a hot dog.

His companions wailed, "YOU . . . YOU ATE . . .
YOU ATE THE . . . YOU ATE THE BATON!"
And in frustration they began to chase him around the rink.

"Tag!" cried Tacky. He loved nothing better than a good game of tag.

So he skated faster. And faster. And fasterandfaster and barreled across the finish line in record time.

29

But wait.

Had Team Nice Icy Land really won?

Did Tacky have the baton?

Without the baton, Team Nice Icy Land would be disqualified.

Out came the medics.

Off went Tacky on the stretcher and under the eye of the big
X-ray machine.

They X-rayed his bottom portion.
Nope, nothing there.

They X-rayed his top.
Certainly nothing there.

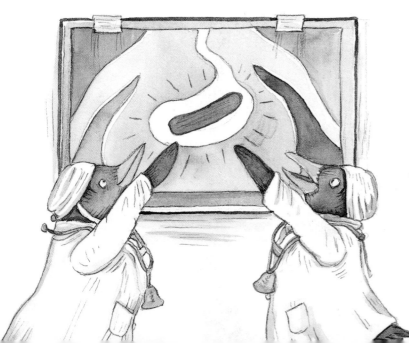

They X-rayed his middle.
And, YES! There it was.

Goodly, Lovely, Angel, Neatly, and Perfect hugged Tacky.
Tacky was an odd bird, but a nice bird to have around.